JANINA DOMANSKA

KING KRAKUS
AND THE DRAGON

GREENWILLOW BOOKS
A DIVISION OF WILLIAM MORROW & COMPANY, INC. / NEW YORK

Library of Congress Cataloging in Publication Data Domanska, Janina. King Krakus and the dragon.
Summary: The people of Krakow are terrified by a dragon until the shoemaker's apprentice devises a plan to rid the town of the monster. [1. Folklore—Poland] I. Title. PZ8.1.D717Ki [398.2] [E] 78-12934 ISBN 0-688-80189-7 ISBN 0-688-84189-9 lib. bdg.

FOR ADA SHEARON WITH LOVE

Long ago, in Poland, where the Vistula flows, there was a mighty forest. King Krakus journeyed to see this distant part of his land. He was so impressed by the beauty of the mountains he decided to build his capital on Wavel, one of the highest peaks. First he had a wooden castle built, and then the peasants began to build the town. They named it Krakow, after the king.

It was a very small town at first, but soon it began to grow. A fine shoemaker came to live there, as well as two blacksmiths, a butcher and a seamstress. Each morning the roosters announced the coming of day. Then the king gave the order to wake the town. A watchman called the hour from Wavel Peak, and the king sat down to his breakfast of barley soup and dumplings.

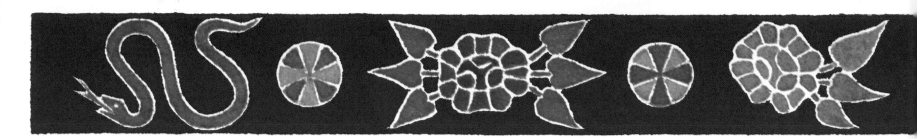

At twilight the night watchman called, "Time to sleep and all sleep well." There was no finer life in the whole world. Whenever the King appeared, everybody kneeled and called, "Long live the king! Long live the princess!" For the king, who was a widower, had a lovely daughter called Wanda. Her eyes were as blue as bottles and she always wore a wreath of flowers in her hair. The king greeted everybody warmly, man, woman and child.

One day a young boy came to the house of the shoemaker. The boy's name was Dratevka, and he was an orphan. The shoemaker asked him to stay and learn the trade. Dratevka worked hard and in two years became an expert. He made a lovely pair of red leather boots and embroidered them with golden horseshoes. The shoemaker said they were fit for a princess, and sent him to the castle.

And so Dratevka brought the boots to Princess Wanda. She was pleased to have them and praised Dratevka for his work. It was spring, white blossoms covered the trees, and Dratevka ran all the way home.

But that midnight the town was awakened by a thunderous noise. Everyone jumped out of bed. The king cried, "The enemy is coming! Get me my sword! My armor!" The townsmen came running with their bows and arrows. At the foot of the mountain the Vistula was hidden by flames and smoke.

A frightful monster, with a long neck, lay sprawled on the shore, swilling water. It was a thousand meters long, had sharp pointed teeth, four thick short legs, and it was covered with scales. Flames sprang from its great jaws and black clouds of smoke came from its nostrils. When it had finished drinking, it roared so that the mountain shook, "I own this mountain, Krakus. I will devour every living thing. I will sit on your throne, and reign in your place. You and your daughter must die."

I t is you who must die!" King Krakus cried out. And flourishing his sword, he ran down the mountainside to fight the dragon. But the dragon spouted a cloud of poisoned smoke, and the brave king fell to the ground.

His people carried him to the palace, where the princess cared for him, and he soon recovered. But the dragon did not leave the riverbank.

Now the townspeople lived in fear. The elders of the town sat in council day and night. Krakow must be freed of the dragon. But how? They did not know what to do.

eanwhile, each morning, the dragon roared to be fed. The townspeople brought him a ram, but soon he was not satisfied with only one. He went into the fields and carried away great numbers of rams, cows and lambs.

L ike everyone else, Dratevka thought a long time about how to save the town. At last he had an idea. He called all the shoemakers together and asked them for tar. Then he asked the coopers and the blacksmiths for bags of sulfur. He asked the butcher for a ram's skin. And from the seamstress he got a needle and thread. Then he went to the king and told him his plan. The king approved. Dratevka took the ram's skin, stuffed it with the tar and sulfur, and stitched it up.

That night he took the stuffed ram down to the river. Dratevka hammered four sticks into the ground. He set the false ram on the wooden legs. He made horns for the ram from two branches. When the dragon awoke in the morning, he saw Dratevka's ram and roared, "There's a fat ram! Just in time! I will have a good breakfast!"
And he swallowed the ram in one gulp.

Soon the dragon began to feel uncomfortable. His stomach grew hotter and hotter. He rushed down to the river to drink. He drank all day and all night. But the sulfur burned in his stomach, and the water could not cool it.

The people gathered to watch him drink.
King Krakus himself came down to the river.
The dragon drank for two weeks without stopping.
The Vistula was almost empty. Suddenly there was a terrible sound. The dragon had burst into a thousand pieces!

Everybody was overjoyed and shouted, "Long live Dratevka!" The king embraced him and appointed him court shoemaker. And, of course, the first pair of boots Dratevka made were for Princess Wanda. They were soft and beautiful, and they were made of dragon skin.